I love you, Sis

_____

_____
DATE

SPIDER SISTERS

by JOHN TRENT, Ph.D.
Illustrated by JUDY LOVE

WORD PUBLISHING
Dallas · London · Vancouver · Melbourne

Spider Sisters

Text copyright © 1996 by John Trent, Ph.D.

Illustrations copyright © 1996 by Judy Love.

Photography: David Caras

Managing Editor: Laura Minchew

Project Editor: Beverly Phillips

Typography: Kelli Hagen

Library of Congress Cataloging-in-Publication Data

Trent, John
   Spider sisters/ by John Trent; illustrated by Judy Love.
     p. cm.
   "Word kids!"
   Summary: A spider tells all the reasons that she loves her sister.
   ISBN 0-8499-1211-3
   [1. Sisters-Fiction. 2. Spiders- Fiction. 3. Christian life- Fiction. 4. Stories in rhyme.]
I. Love, Judy, 1953-   ill.   II. Title
   PZ8.3. T693Sp 1996
   [E]—dc20   96-7358
                                                    CIP
                                                     AC

Printed in the United States of America

96 97 98 99 00 LBM 9 8 7 6 5 4 3 2 1

To our two precious daughters . . .
they are "spider sisters" who love each other so much
and live out this book . . .

LAURA
(your turn to go first this time)

and

KARI.

—Dad and Mom (JOHN AND CINDY TRENT)

This book is dedicated
to my five sisters but especially to JAN, my twin,
with whom I have shared so much
from the very beginning of our life together.

—JUDY LOVE

My sister is a spider and that's quite all right with me,
For she has eight arms and legs to share her dolls and toys, you see.

Oh, I know that she's not perfect and at times we *fuss and fight,*
But for a million special reasons, she is more than just all right.

There are lots of sisters who talk and talk, wherever they may go,
But we SPEAK a language we made up and only we two know.

That way when we're at school or even riding on the bus,
We use our "secret" sister language no one knows but us.

And it's not just "secret" sister talks that make me feel so loved,
It's that very special way she gives me "spider sister" **hugs**.

They're the kind of hugs that cheer you on a really crummy day,
For those **fuzzy** arms say "You're still special" more than words could say.

If you think I love my sister, then you're right in what you hear,
For she's full of fun and giggles, and always has a listening ear.

When I'm sad, she's always there to help me dry my tears,
And when I hit my first home run, she led the loudest cheers.

One summer night while Sis and I were both at home alone,
I shouldn't have, but I listened in while she was on the phone.

I heard Lydia the Ladybug, the most popular girl in school,
Inviting my sister, but not me, to a party at her pool.

My sister could have said, "I'll come and leave my sis at home."
But like a true-blue "spider sister" she spoke **BOLDLY** on the phone.

"If you want me at the party, then I'm coming with my sis.
It's the *two of us* together or your party I must miss."

Well, we did go to the party which was grand in every way,
There were lots of games and friends and cake to mark the special day.

But the thing that meant the most was not the food or games or song,
But the fact my "spider sister" wanted ME to come along.

She's been an awesome sister since the day that we were born,

Even when I ~~tore~~ her favorite shirt I never should have worn.

And it's not that I'm just like her, 'cause that's really not the case,

For she loves to have tea parties, while I love a *game of chase*.

No matter what the season, she is always by my side,

If we're helping Dad rake leaves, or going down the waterslide.

But her favorite thing to do is race behind me on our sled,

Giggling, shouting, playing, waving with our arms held overhead.

You might just think I love her 'cause she's always so much fun,
But the greatest thing she's taught me is to L♡VE like God's own Son.

Like the time that we were playing and I looked up in *shock* to see
That my sister had gone over and was talking to a flea!

Felecia Flea just had to be the least-liked girl in school,
Yet my sister saw how **sad** she looked, and lived "the Golden Rule."

She insisted that Felecia join us in the "mothball" game,
For she always sees God's ☆best☆ in kids and treats them all the same.

Each night when Mama tucks us in and sings our favorite song, ♩♪♩♪♩♪♩♪♪♩♪♩♪♩♪

She gets down on her knees with us, and we both pray along.

Mom asks that God will bless me and He'll bless my sister, too.

And she prays our love for Him will keep us close like superglue.

One day we'll both grow up, and we will move away from home,

And we'll both have loving husbands and cute children of our own.

Then my prayer will be our kids will be as close as we've become,

And they'll each have 🕷 spider sisters 🕷 who both love the other one.

We'll always have each other!